MR. SNOW

by Roger Hargreaves

One night, two days before Christmas, it started to snow.

All night it snowed and snowed and snowed and snowed and snowed.

Millions and billions and trillions of big, white, soft snowflakes covered the whole, wide world.

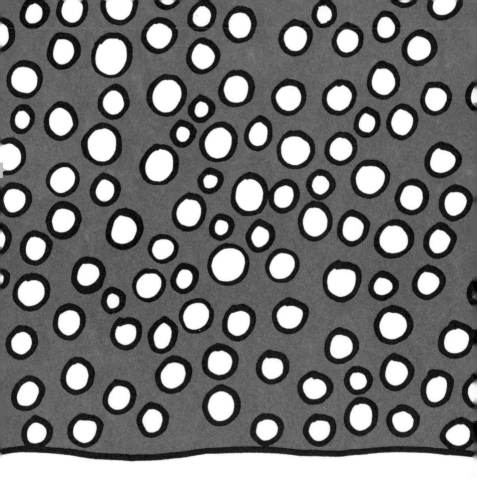

When morning came it was quite amazing to see just how much snow had fallen.

All the houses, all the trees, all the roads and all the fields were covered.

It was almost as if a huge, white blanket had been gently laid over everything.

Everywhere you looked was white!

And then the sun came out!

And so did the children!

They were all dressed up and muffled up, wearing scarves and woollies and gloves and boots so that they wouldn't catch cold.

All the children were so excited to see so much snow, which isn't surprising really because there was more snow than they'd ever seen before.

Some of them went on their sledges, racing down the hills.

Some of them, who didn't have sledges, threw snowballs at each other.

One little boy even made a snowball that was as big as himself.

And some of the children made snowmen!

Then it was Christmas Eve.

The children all went home early so that they could go to bed early so that they could get up early to see what Father Christmas had brought them.

But that particular Christmas Eve, Father Christmas was in trouble.

And the trouble was that it had snowed so much that Father Christmas was stuck.

Well and truly stuck!

There was so much snow that his reindeer simply couldn't pull his sleigh piled high with all the presents that he had to deliver to all the children.

"Oh dear!" thought Father Christmas to himself. "Oh dear me. What am I to do?"

He sat down on his sack of toys and thought and thought how he could manage to deliver all the presents to all the children before they woke up on Christmas morning.

"Oh dear! Oh dear me!" he said out loud, and sighed.

Now, it just so happened that Father Christmas had got himself stuck just beside a snowman which one of the children had built.

And that gave him an idea.

A good idea.

A very good idea.

A very good idea indeed.

"How would you like to help me?" he asked the snowman.

But of course the snowman didn't answer because snowmen can't talk, can they?

"Of course, I'll have to use some of my magic to bring him to life," thought Father Christmas to himself.

So, he tugged his white beard three times and muttered some Father Christmassy magic words into it.

Suddenly, you might almost say magically, the snowman did come to life.

"Hello Father Christmas," said Mr Snow, which was the snowman's name.

"You look a bit sort of stuck if you ask me, which you aren't , but I'll say so anyway, and if you ask me again I'd say you need a sort of helping hand, if you know what I mean, which you probably do, because that's probably why you've brought me to life, which you certainly did, so can I be of any assistance?"

Mr Snow, as you might have gathered, was a rather talkative sort of snowman.

"Exactly!" beamed Father Christmas. "Let's get started!"

And start they did.

Mr Snow gave Father Christmas an enormous push, and off they went.

They divided the work between them.

It was Mr Snow's job to make sure that all the right toys for all the right boys, and all the right toys for all the right girls, were put into all the right sacks.

It was Father Christmas's job to make sure he took all the right sacks down all the right chimneys and delivered all the right toys to all the right boys and all the right toys to all the right girls.

Mr Snow and Father Christmas made sure that Susan got her teddy bear.

Mr Snow and Father Christmas made sure that Peter got his train.

Mr Snow and Father Christmas made sure that John got his piggy bank.

Mr Snow and Father Christmas even made sure that little Jane got her squeaky, pink elephant to play with in the bath.

And then, all of a sudden, they discovered that, between them, they'd finished.

"I'd like to thank you very much indeed for helping me deliver all the right toys to all the right boys," said Father Christmas, shaking Mr Snow by the hand.

"Not forgetting all the right toys to all the right girls," replied Mr Snow, shaking Father Christmas by the hand.

"And now I'd better turn you back into a snowman again," said Father Christmas.

"Thank you again and goodbye!"

"My pleasure!" smiled Mr Snow.

And do you know, from that Christmas to this Christmas, Father Christmas always chooses a snowman to help him.

So the next time you build a snowman, you'd better make sure you build him properly, because somebody you know might want that snowman to give him a hand.

And you know who that would be, don't you?

Fantastic offers for Mr. Men fans!

Collect all your Mr. Men or Little Miss books in these superb durable collectors' cases!
Only £5.99 inc. postage and packing, these wipe-clean, hard-wearing cases will give all your Mr. Men or Little Miss books a beautiful new home!

Keep track of your collection with this giant-sized double-sided Mr. Men and Little Miss Collectors' poster.
Collect 6 tokens and we will send you a brilliant giant-sized double-sided collectors' poster! Simply tape a £1 coin to cover postage and packaging in the space provided and fill out the form overleaf.

STICK £1 COIN HERE
(for poster only)

Only need a few Mr. Men or Little Miss to complete your set? You can order any of the titles on the back of the books from our Mr. Men order line on 0870 787 1724. Orders should be delivered between 5 and 7 working days.

--- **TO BE COMPLETED BY AN ADULT** ---

To apply for any of these great offers, ask an adult to complete the details below and send this whole page with the appropriate payment and tokens, to: MR. MEN CLASSIC OFFER, PO BOX 715, HORSHAM RH12 5WG

☐ Please send me a giant-sized double-sided collectors' poster.
AND ☐ I enclose 6 tokens and have taped a £1 coin to the other side of this page.

☐ Please send me ☐ Mr. Men Library case(s) and/or ☐ Little Miss library case(s) at £5.99 each inc P&P

☐ I enclose a cheque/postal order payable to Egmont UK Limited for £...................

OR ☐ Please debit my MasterCard / Visa / Maestro / Delta account (delete as appropriate) for £...................

Card no. ☐☐☐☐ ☐☐☐☐ ☐☐☐☐ ☐☐☐☐ ☐☐☐☐   Security code ☐☐☐

Issue no. (if available) ☐   Start Date ☐☐/☐☐/☐☐   Expiry Date ☐☐/☐☐/☐☐

Fan's name: Date of birth:

Address:
....

.... Postcode:

Name of parent / guardian:

Email for parent / guardian:

Signature of parent / guardian:

Please allow 28 days for delivery. Offer is only available while stocks last. We reserve the right to change the terms of this offer at any time and we offer a 14 day money back guarantee. This does not affect your statutory rights. Offers apply to UK only.

☐ We may occasionally wish to send you information about other Egmont children's books.
If you would rather we didn't, please tick this box.   **Ref: MRM 001**